DISCARD

Key
VOTING LAWS

LAWS
THAT CHANGED
HISTORY

Alex Acks

Cavendish Square
New York

Published in 2020 by Cavendish Square Publishing, LLC

243 5th Avenue, Suite 136, New York, NY 10016

Copyright © 2020 by Cavendish Square Publishing, LLC

First Edition

No part of this publication may be reproduced, stored in a retrieval system, or transmitted in any form or by any means—electronic, mechanical, photocopying, recording, or otherwise—without the prior permission of the copyright owner. Request for permission should be addressed to Permissions, Cavendish Square Publishing, 243 5th Avenue, Suite 136, New York, NY 10016. Tel (877) 980-4450; fax (877) 980-4454.

Website: cavendishsq.com

This publication represents the opinions and views of the author based on his or her personal experience, knowledge, and research. The information in this book serves as a general guide only. The author and publisher have used their best efforts in preparing this book and disclaim liability rising directly or indirectly from the use and application of this book.

All websites were available and accurate when this book was sent to press.

Cataloging-in-Publication Data

Names: Acks, Alex.
Title: Key voting laws / Alex Acks.
Description: New York : Cavendish Square Publishing, 2020. | Series: Laws that changed history | Includes glossary and index.
Identifiers: ISBN 9781502655356 (pbk.) | ISBN 9781502655363 (library bound) | ISBN 9781502655370 (ebook)
Subjects: LCSH: Suffrage--United States--Juvenile literature. | Election law--United States--Juvenile literature. | Voting--United States--Juvenile literature. | Voter registration--United States--Juvenile literature. | Voting--Corrupt practices--United States--Juvenile literature. | Women--Suffrage--United States--Juvenile literature.
Classification: LCC KF4891.A29 2020 | DDC 342.73'072--dc23

Printed in China

Photo Credits: Cover, p. 1 Frederic J. Brown/AFP/Getty Images; pp. 6–7 National Geographic Image Collection/Alamy Stock Photo; pp. 9, 49 Library of Congress Prints and Photographs Division; pp. 11, 14–15, 42 Everett Historical/Shutterstock.com; p. 18 Print Collector/Hulton Archive/Getty Images; pp. 20–21, 38–39 Bettmann/Getty Images; p. 23 Stock Montage/Archive Photos/Getty Images; pp. 24–25 Universal History Archive/Universal Images Group/Getty Images; pp. 28–29 Underwood Archives/Archive Photos/Getty Images; pp. 32–33 Sundry Photography/Shutterstock.com; p. 34 Ed Clark/The LIFE Images Collection/Getty Images; p. 44 DNetromphotos/Shutterstock.com; p. 47 © AP Images; p. 51 Rob Crandall/Shutterstock.com; p. 53 Mark Wilson/Getty Images; p. 56 Ronnie21/Shutterstock.com; p. 58 Tasos Katopodis/Getty Images; p. 60 George Frey/Getty Images; cover, back cover, and interior pages Capitol dome graphic Alexkava/Shutterstock.com.

CONTENTS

Introduction 4

CHAPTER 1
Foundational Voting Laws 6

CHAPTER 2
(Almost) Universal Male Suffrage 14

CHAPTER 3
Women Win the Right to Vote 22

CHAPTER 4
Voter Suppression 31

CHAPTER 5
What Do You Mean, They Couldn't Vote? 41

CHAPTER 6
Voting in Modern America 48

CHAPTER 7
What Is the Future of the Vote? 55

CHRONOLOGY 62

CHAPTER NOTES 65

GLOSSARY 75

FURTHER READING 76

INDEX 78

Introduction

On January 8, 2019, 1.5 million people in Florida who hadn't been allowed to register to vote on January 7 could turn in their voter registration forms. Just two months before, voters in the state passed Amendment Four with nearly 65 percent of the vote. Amendment Four changed Florida's constitution to "restore the right to vote for people with prior felony convictions, except those convicted of murder or a felony sexual offense, upon completion of their sentences, including prison, parole, and probation."[1]

If you've never been convicted of a crime or known someone who has been, you may not have thought about what a conviction can do to voting rights. In America, there are only two states that don't place at least some restrictions on the voting rights of people who have been convicted of a felony: Maine and Vermont. Most other states do not allow people who are currently in prison to vote, though they vary on whether felons are allowed to vote again once they are on parole or probation.

INTRODUCTION

As of 2019, there are three states where anyone who has any kind of felony conviction permanently loses their right to vote: Iowa, Kentucky, and Virginia.[2] Florida was the fourth state on that list until the passage of Amendment Four.

Many laws that take away the rights of people convicted of felonies can trace their lineage back to the end of the US Civil War. Former Confederate states began to put "black codes" in place; these were laws that placed restrictions on employment for black people and instituted high fines for breaking those laws. Those who couldn't pay off their fines—and most couldn't—were effectively enslaved again to work off their debt under a white employer. As early as 1894 and continuing through the Jim Crow era, when racial segregation was law in the South and was enforced socially rather than legally in many places in the North, criminal codes were revisited as a way to disenfranchise black voters. States across the country passed laws that took the right to vote away from anyone who committed even a minor crime, and black people were targeted disproportionately for arrest, sometimes for false charges. One arrest could lead to a person losing their right to vote forever.[3] The Florida law that Amendment Four overturned originated in 1868.

One of the dynamos who helped change that law was Desmond Meade, a fifty-one-year-old black man who had lost his right to vote after a felony conviction. In 2005, Meade was on the brink of committing suicide after finishing a three-year prison sentence that left him addicted to drugs, unemployed, and homeless. Instead, he checked himself into a rehabilitation center and began taking community college classes that led him to Florida International University Law School. He wasn't allowed to take the bar exam because of his conviction, but he used his legal knowledge to figure out how to best challenge Florida's voting law. On January 8, 2019, Desmond Meade registered to vote.[4]

CHAPTER 1

Foundational Voting Laws

Elections are nothing new in the world. Thousands of years ago in ancient Athens, male citizens voted on all of the issues that affected the cities they lived in. A great statesman of the time, Pericles, said that Athenians thought of "a man who takes no interest in public affairs not as apathetic, but as completely useless." Women, children, enslaved people, and foreigners were not allowed to vote.[1]

The kind of elections we're familiar with today started developing during the 1600s in America and Europe, driven

FOUNDATIONAL VOTING LAWS

In ancient Greece, male citizens voted regularly on issues that affected their cities. Women, children, enslaved people, and foreigners were not allowed to vote.

by a new political idea that individuals, rather than estates or companies, mattered and should be counted and represented.[2] Elections had existed in England since 1265, but the British Bill of Rights of 1689 established that elections should be held regularly and be free, meaning that anyone who had the right to vote should be able to exercise that right without interference.[3] At that time, "anyone" meant men who owned property of a certain value—a tiny percentage of the population.

Elections in colonial America were modeled on the colonists' knowledge and experience from Europe. On July 30, 1619, a representative assembly of Virginia's corporations and plantations met in Jamestown. From then on, that form of government spread through the other colonies. Each colony decided who was allowed to vote, which generally meant white, male property owners over the age of twenty-one.[4] There were exceptions; some colonies allowed unmarried and widowed women to vote, or free black men—if they met the property requirements.

While there were many factors that led to the Revolutionary War, a major complaint of the colonists was "taxation without representation." The colonists were being taxed to pay for English war debt by a Parliament they were not allowed to vote for. As limited as the franchise was at that time, its power was still undeniable.[5]

Voting at the Dawn of America

The American Revolutionary War began at Lexington and Concord on April 19, 1775, with "the shot heard round the world" and didn't end until 1783. The Constitutional Convention began drafting the Constitution of the United States of America on May 14, 1787, and the new government began two years later on March 4, 1789. There still needed to be a government in that intervening time.

FOUNDATIONAL VOTING LAWS

After the Declaration of Independence, the Second Continental Congress spent the next year and a half debating and creating the Articles of Confederation, which were sent to the states on November 15, 1777. After all thirteen of the new states ratified the document, it went into effect on March 1, 1781. The government created by the Articles of Confederation was much weaker than the one we have now because the former colonists feared and disliked the idea of a strong central government. Because of this, the new government had barely enough power to run the war, and that lack of power—which included an inability to get money from the states—was what caused the Articles of Confederation to fail and made the US Constitution necessary.[6]

Under the Articles of Confederation, each state had only one vote in the legislature, though a state would have at least two delegates in Congress. These delegates were elected by state legislatures.[7] The matter of elections and whether people ought to be able to vote for members of Congress was a topic of hot debate during the drafting of the Articles. Roger Sherman of Connecticut didn't want there to be direct voting, saying, "The people should

James Madison, who would later go on to be the United States' fourth president, said that regulating voting required a "particular delicacy."

9

KEY VOTING LAWS

have as little to do as may be about the government. They lack information and are constantly liable to be misled."[8]

In contrast, James Madison argued, "The right to suffrage is a fundamental Article in Republican Constitutions. The regulation of it is, at the same time, a task of peculiar delicacy. Allow the right exclusively to property, and the rights of persons may be oppressed … Extend it equally to all, and the rights of property or the claims of justice may be overruled by a majority without property, or interested in measures of injustice."[9]

Ultimately, the Articles of Confederation passed on the matter of elections, leaving their running and questions of who should or should not be able to vote up to the states. When the Constitution was drafted, it, too, left elections to the states, though this time the Founders reserved the right of a future Congress to make laws regarding elections: "The times, places and manner of holding elections for Senators and Representatives, shall be prescribed in each state by the legislature thereof; but the Congress may at any time by law make or alter such regulations."[10]

The Laws Give and the Laws Take

Once the Constitution went into effect, voting was mostly limited by the states to white men over the age of twenty-one who owned property and were of a Protestant faith. That was about 6 percent of the population at the time.[11] However, since voting regulations were controlled by the states, there were exceptions to the rule.

Some states allowed Revolutionary War veterans to vote, whether they owned property or not. Unmarried and widowed women had been able to vote in New York, New Hampshire, and Massachusetts during colonial times, and they continued to do so under the Articles of Confederation until state laws changed, shortly before the US Constitution went into effect. The New

FOUNDATIONAL VOTING LAWS

Women have always fought to be allowed to vote. Here, members of the League of Women Voters advocate for women to get involved in the democratic process in 1924, four years after women gained the right to vote nationally.

Jersey state constitution didn't actually specify gender in its voting requirements, so property-owning women were able to vote. New Jersey even changed its state laws to acknowledge that women could vote in 1790. Then, seventeen years later, it took the right to vote away with another law.[12]

Free black people were allowed to vote in New Jersey if they owned property until the state constitution was changed to restrict the vote to only white men.[13] In Pennsylvania, black men were allowed to vote until 1838.[14] Because the right to vote was left entirely to the states, it could be given or taken away by legislative whim.

11

KEY VOTING LAWS

Religious Tests

Article VI of the United States Constitution says that "no religious Test shall ever be required as a Qualification to any Office of public Trust under the United States." In contrast, the government of England had a variety of Test Acts that excluded people who were not members of the Church of England from office. The US Constitution strictly forbade that kind of religious exclusion from happening in the United States—but only for federal office. This ban on religious tests did not extend to voting rights, which were left up to the states. Several colonies and then states excluded Jewish or Catholic people from voting until those laws were eliminated by 1790.

The Naturalization Act of 1790

The Constitution uses "citizen" versus "person" quite deliberately—and it made citizenship a condition of holding federal public office. However, citizenship was not actually defined in the US Constitution as a requirement to vote. Initially, many states allowed noncitizens to vote; until the 1920s, forty different states and territories allowed noncitizen voting in at least some elections. Being a white, male property owner was considered to be the most important factor, and allowing noncitizens who met those requirements to vote was seen as a way to lure desirable immigrants to the United States. Shifting immigrant demographics and broadening state voting laws (such as the elimination of property requirements) led to states eliminating the ability of noncitizens to vote.[15]

The question of citizenship was not inextricably linked with voting rights in early America—rather, the property, gender, and racial requirements set by states were much more important. However, as more states began to require citizenship in order to vote, the question of who could become a citizen made a difference.

The Naturalization Act of 1790 was the first set of rules in the United States about which immigrants could become citizens. Free white people of "good character" could become naturalized citizens; white indentured servants and people of color were excluded. Most women were also excluded, although there were certain exceptions. In addition to providing proof of good character, aspiring citizens had to live in the United States for at least two years, take an oath to support the Constitution, and formally renounce their citizenship of the country they were born in.[16] Over the next eight years, further Naturalization Acts extended that residency requirement up to fourteen years—and kept citizenship limited to free white people.

CHAPTER 2

(Almost) Universal Male Suffrage

Over time, property requirements for white men to vote began to loosen. Some transformed into proof of a certain amount of nonproperty assets, or to a tax-paying requirement. States that were on the frontier at the time were more interested in universal (white) male suffrage, perhaps in the interest of attracting more men to their territory. Vermont and Kentucky joined the Union in 1791 and 1792 respectively, and neither required even tax-paying to vote. This set a pattern for new states joining and may have encouraged the older states to ease requirements more. In 1856, North Carolina became the last state to eliminate property requirements for voting, and by the time of the American Civil War, only a few states still had tax-paying requirements.[1]

(ALMOST) UNIVERSAL MALE SUFFRAGE

Shown here is Abraham Lincoln visiting Civil War soldiers. At that time, Native Americans, black people, and all women still could not vote.

KEY VOTING LAWS

While white male suffrage was almost universal by the Civil War, most people were still not allowed to vote, including people of color and white women. These excluded people as well as white men who believed in equality for all, such as Quakers, fought to expand the right to vote. State laws could be frequently changed; the best and most lasting way to guarantee the vote for anyone was to amend the US Constitution.

The Thirteenth and Fourteenth Amendments

The US Civil War officially began with the attack on Fort Sumter in South Carolina by the Confederate military on April 12, 1861. A few months earlier, on December 20, 1860, South Carolina had become the first state to secede from the Union. In its declaration of secession, South Carolina mentioned the failure of the federal government to enforce the Fugitive Slave Acts and the overall hostility of nonslave states and the national government toward slavery. By the middle of 1861, ten other states had seceded, and many, including Texas, Georgia, and Mississippi, cited the need to continue slavery among their reasons.[2]

The Civil War ended about four years later, when Confederate general Robert E. Lee surrendered at Appomattox Court House to Union general Ulysses S. Grant on April 9, 1865. Months before the war ended, Congress passed the Thirteenth Amendment to the Constitution, abolishing slavery. The Thirteenth Amendment had to be ratified by three-quarters of the states before it could take effect. Pressure from Andrew Johnson, newly made president in the wake of Abraham Lincoln's assassination, got the necessary number of Southern states to ratify the amendment, with Georgia as the twenty-seventh state pushing it over the finish line on December 6, 1865.[3] Other Southern states took longer;

Mississippi didn't fully ratify the Thirteenth Amendment until 2013.[4]

President Lincoln had at least been willing to broach the idea of suffrage for black men; he wrote to the newly elected governor of Louisiana on the topic prior to the state ratifying the Thirteenth Amendment. However, he couldn't follow through with this idea, as he was assassinated three days later.

President Andrew Johnson proved to be recalcitrant as Reconstruction began. He initially seemed to approve of the idea of the vote for black men, but he made no move to intervene as more Southern states specifically denied black voting rights and began to put restrictive black codes into place that attempted to make formerly enslaved people back into slaves in all but name. When he attempted to veto the Civil Rights Act of 1866, which declared all people—except Native Americans—born in the United States citizens, part of his justification was

The Reconstruction Act of 1867

After overriding Andrew Johnson's veto of the Civil Rights Act of 1866, Congress overrode another veto by President Johnson in 1867, saving the Reconstruction Acts over his protests. These acts divided the South (except for Tennessee) into five military districts and required that all of the Southern states make new constitutions that had to include suffrage for all men, regardless of race. The new state constitutions had to be approved by Congress.

Often protected by federal troops, nearly half a million black men in the South exercised their right to vote, giving black men a seat in Congress for the first time. The state of Mississippi even elected two black senators before Reconstruction ended in 1877.[5]

KEY VOTING LAWS

In 1866, President Andrew Johnson was not convinced that black men should have the right to vote, but Congress disagreed with him.

an attack on black people voting: "Four million of them have just emerged from slavery into freedom. Can it be reasonably supposed that they possess the requisite qualifications to entitle them to all the privileges and equalities of the citizens of the United States?"[6]

Congress overrode Johnson's veto, but it had become apparent that a constitutional amendment bestowing citizenship was necessary—it was too easy for a law to be repealed. Representative Thaddeus Stevens introduced a constitutional amendment in April 1866; by June it was sent to the states. Over the resistance of President Johnson and the Southern states, Congress pushed the citizenship amendment through by making its ratification, and that of the Thirteenth Amendment, a requirement for Southern states to have representation in Washington again.

On July 9, 1868, the Fourteenth Amendment hit its required number of states with Louisiana and South Carolina. The Fourteenth Amendment declared that all people who were born in the United States were citizens, and therefore had all of the rights thereof. Further, it said that states who denied eligible male inhabitants the right to vote would be punished with reduced representation in Congress—though eligibility was still a matter for the states.[7] The Fourteenth Amendment showed that the federal government now had an interest in helping people exercise their right to vote.

The Fifteenth Amendment

While states in the South were being forced to put universal male suffrage into their state constitutions, in 1868 only eight states of the abolitionist North allowed black men to vote. There was also a massive shift about to happen in how representation would work in Congress. With slavery ended, the "three-fifths" compromise of the original US Constitution, which said each

KEY VOTING LAWS

The Fifteenth Amendment to the Constitution ensured that black men got the vote, meaning that—at least on paper—their right to vote was guaranteed. Shown here is an illustration of black men lining up to vote.

black slave counted as three-fifths of a person, also ended. Southern states gained a massive population boost overnight, giving them more representatives in Congress—which made the votes of black men, or the suppression thereof, very important to the political parties. Republican politicians feared an influx of Democrats and felt they could count on the support of black voters. The answer to their trouble seemed to be to ensure that black men in the North and Midwest could vote as well.

The Fifteenth Amendment was passed during the lame duck session of Congress in 1869 and sent to the states to ratify because Congress knew there were enough Republican-controlled state legislatures still in session to see the amendment through. Radical Republicans wanted the amendment to ban literacy tests and property qualifications for voting as well as racial requirements for holding office; the moderate compromise sent to the states lacked those provisions.

Thirteen months later, after much uncertainty at the state level, the Fifteenth Amendment became law on March 30, 1870.[8] The amendment simply states, "The right of citizens of the United States to vote shall not be denied or abridged by the United States or by any State on account of race, color, or previous condition of servitude."

At least on paper, the voting rights of nonwhite citizens (which at the time referred only to black men) were guaranteed.

CHAPTER 3

Women Win the Right to Vote

Women in the United States have never been passive or shy about wanting equal rights. On March 31, 1776, Abigail Adams wrote to her husband, future president John Adams, "And, by the way, in the new code of laws which I suppose it will be necessary for you to make, I desire you would remember the ladies and be more generous and favorable to them than your ancestors. Do not put such unlimited power into the hands of the husbands. Remember, all men would be tyrants if they could. If particular care and attention is not paid to the ladies, we are determined to foment a rebellion, and will not hold ourselves bound by any laws in which we have no voice or representation."[1]

The women were, at best, forgotten in the US Constitution, and at worst were outright ignored. States that had, as colonies, allowed at least property-owning women to vote took that right away not long after the United States came into existence as its own country. Less than a century later, as Abigail Adams had threatened, the ladies did "foment a rebellion."

WOMEN WIN THE RIGHT TO VOTE

First Lady Abigail Adams asked her husband, John, to remember the women during his work planning the new government of the United States. She was never shy about pressing for equal rights.

KEY VOTING LAWS

The Seneca Falls Convention

From July 19 to 20, 1848, a convention was held in Seneca Falls, New York. Advertised as a "convention to discuss the social, civil, and religious conditions and rights of woman," the Seneca Falls Convention became the first women's rights convention to be held in the United States.

The convention was organized by local female Quakers in cooperation with Elizabeth Cady Stanton. Stanton was active in the abolitionist movement with her husband, Henry Brewster Stanton, who cofounded the Republican Party.[2]

The Seneca Falls Convention covered multiple discussions about women in society and saw the unveiling of the Declaration of Sentiments, a document that mimicked the Declaration of Independence and sought to correct the ways women had been left out of society. Out of the 300 people in attendance, 100 signed the declaration—68 women and 32 men. Accompanying the declaration were eleven resolutions; only the ninth was not unanimously adopted. It read, "*Resolved*, That it is the duty of the women of this country to secure to themselves their sacred right to the elective franchise."[3]

The debate that followed over that resolution covered many attendees' concerns that women seeking the right to vote would detract from the other resolutions, which largely dealt with the place of women in society and inequality of laws. Stanton would not back down

WOMEN WIN THE RIGHT TO VOTE

In 1920, women gathered at the Republican National Convention, insisting on the same thing Elizabeth Cady Stanton had advocated for fifty years before: the right to vote.

25

on her support for the right to vote, and Frederick Douglass, a free black man who was committed to abolition and women's suffrage, helped her in convincing the convention to pass the resolution.[4] Women had their sights set on the vote.

State by State

Twenty years after the Seneca Falls Convention, the Fourteenth Amendment was ratified. While a triumph for abolitionists, it added the first explicit mention of gender into the US Constitution: "But when the right to vote in any election … is denied to any of the male inhabitants of such State …" This statement that only men were voters led to a major split among the people who were activists for both abolition and women's rights. Elizabeth Cady Stanton, still a leading activist for the vote and other rights of women, stated, "If the word 'male' be inserted, it will take us a century at least to get it out."

When it came to the Fifteenth Amendment, the schism turned ugly. Stanton and Susan B. Anthony, another abolitionist and leader in the women's rights movement, wanted the Fifteenth Amendment to include women as well, and not just affirm the right of black *men* to vote.[5] Activists such as Lucy Stone, who believed in both abolition and women's suffrage, feared that if women were added to the Fifteenth Amendment, it would not be ratified at all, which would keep black men oppressed. Frederick Douglass disagreed publicly with Stanton; he believed that black men needed voting rights first because they faced so much prejudice and violence.[6]

As ratification proceeded, it brought out the racist side of the fight for women's suffrage. Stanton stated that black men weren't ready for the vote in a rant that involved racial slurs.[7] Other white women in the suffrage movement, such as Stone, stood with black women such as Sojourner Truth and Ida B.

Wells-Barnett, dedicating themselves to the cause of securing the vote for all women—not just white women.[8]

The Fifteenth Amendment fight led to a split in the efforts of the suffrage movement. Anti-Fifteenth activists Stanton and Anthony founded the National Woman Suffrage Association (NWSA) in 1869, an organization that was fixated on getting a federal constitutional amendment. By 1878, NWSA was able to lobby Congress enough to get it to form study committees; however, when the amendment those committees produced made it to the Senate floor in 1886, it was voted down.

Also in 1869, Lucy Stone cofounded the American Woman Suffrage Association (AWSA) with other activists who had supported the Fifteenth Amendment and focused instead on a

The Direct Election of Senators

When the Constitution was written in 1787, state legislatures were given the task of electing US senators. Legislatures sometimes deadlocked on senator votes, which meant a position in the Senate might be left vacant for months or even years. In some states, political parties so thoroughly ran the government that senators were dismissed as puppets of the party machine.

In the 1890s, the House began to propose the direct election of senators, which the Senate pointedly ignored. In 1911, another resolution on direct election passed the House, with a "race rider" that prevented the government from intervening in voter racial discrimination cases. The Senate removed the rider and approved the resolution. By April 8, 1913, three-quarters of the states had ratified the Seventeenth Amendment, so from then on, people could directly vote for their senators.[9]

KEY VOTING LAWS

state-by-state strategy. That same year, AWSA won its first victory when Wyoming Territory granted women the right to vote. Women's suffrage stayed in the Wyoming State Constitution when the state was admitted into the Union in 1890.

The two organizations came back together in 1890 to form the National American Woman Suffrage Association (NAWSA) and continue the state-by-state strategy under the guidance of Stone, Stanton, and Anthony. By 1896, Colorado, Utah, and Idaho had given women the right to vote in their state constitutions. By 1918, with NAWSA now under the leadership of Carrie Chapman Catt, seventeen more states and territories, mostly in the West, had given women the right to vote.[10]

The Nineteenth Amendment

As the 1800s gave way to the 1900s, the argument for women's suffrage shifted to the idea that women deserved the vote because they would make different and superior legislative decisions. The temperance movement, which aimed to ban alcohol in the United States, pushed for suffrage because women were thought to be strongly anti-alcohol.[11] White supremacists such as Belle Kearney made a far more racist appeal, arguing that suffrage would ensure and codify white supremacy via elections. People who shared Kearney's views wanted only white women to be allowed to vote.[12]

WOMEN WIN THE RIGHT TO VOTE

Women voted across the United States for the first time in 1920, though many individual states had given women voting rights in their state constitutions years before.

The day before the inauguration of President Woodrow Wilson, March 3, 1913, more than 5,000 women, including radical activist Helen Keller, marched in Washington, DC, to demand the right to vote.[13] President Wilson was no ally to the suffrage movement, but he was also not immune to pressure. Militant activists of the National Woman's Party staged demonstrations and picketed the White House. The protests started peaceful but eventually became violent; women were arrested and continued protesting in jail through hunger strikes. When President Wilson found out about the protesters being force-fed in prison, he changed his stance and joined his daughter, suffragette Jessie Woodrow Wilson Sayre, in supporting a constitutional amendment. His first public endorsement of women's suffrage came in a speech before Congress in 1918, when he said the efforts of women during the First World War had earned them the right to vote.

With personal lobbying from President Wilson and the continued efforts of suffrage activists, the Nineteenth Amendment was passed by Congress on June 4, 1919, and sent to the states. President Wilson later said of the amendment, "I deem it one of the greatest honors of my life that this great event, so stoutly fought for, for so many years, should have occurred during the period of my administration."[14]

Most of the Southern states rejected the Nineteenth Amendment, which enjoyed strong support in the North, West, and Midwest. The ratification came down to Tennessee, and then down to one man: Representative Harry T. Burn. Burn initially opposed the amendment until his own mother personally lobbied him. On August 18, 1920, he cast the deciding vote, and the Nineteenth Amendment was ratified. On November 2 of that year, more than 8 million women voted in elections across the United States for the first time.[15]

Chapter 4

Voter Suppression

With the passage of the Fourteenth and Fifteenth Amendments, male citizens of all races could theoretically vote. With the passage of the Nineteenth Amendment in 1920, female citizens of all races could vote as well. The reality of voting was different from the laws on the books, however. The administration of elections was still left wholly to the states. As soon as voting rights were granted by the federal government, states moved to block them with legal tricks. This suppression of the vote raised a question that still haunts modern America: Does someone really have the right to vote if that person is prevented from casting a ballot?

Jim Crow Laws

As soon as post–Civil War Reconstruction began, Southern states began to pass laws to restrict the rights and freedoms of no-longer-enslaved black people. While black people were temporarily protected by federal troops during the ten-year

KEY VOTING LAWS

Voter suppression has made a resurgence in recent years, with Republicans generally leading the charge with tricks such as gerrymandering (redistricting), voter purges, and voter ID laws.

period of Radical Reconstruction between 1867 and 1877, once the troops were gone and Republicans no longer had total control of the government, the Southern states had free rein.

Starting in the 1890s, these states began to pass laws that mandated segregation, legally forcing people of color to use inferior public services and occupy inferior public spaces. For example, drinking fountains were labeled either "whites only" or "coloreds only," and if a nonwhite person was caught using the wrong drinking fountain, they could be legally punished. Additionally, they often faced socially enforced harassment and violence. These laws became known as Jim Crow laws, after a racist insult that was used against black people.[1]

When a Jim Crow law from Louisiana was challenged under the equal protection clause of the Fourteenth Amendment, which states that all citizens are to be equally protected by the laws of the country, the Supreme Court confirmed in *Plessy v. Ferguson* (1896) that segregation was allowed as long as accommodations were "equal, but separate."[2] This racist doctrine became known

KEY VOTING LAWS

Under Jim Crow laws, in order to cast a vote, a voter often had to pay a poll tax. This meant a good portion of voters could not vote, given that they were too poor to pay what was asked.

as "separate but equal" and persisted for almost sixty years, until Chief Justice Earl Warren wrote in *Brown v. Board of Education of Topeka* (1954) that "separate educational facilities are inherently unequal."[3]

Jim Crow laws didn't just seek to restrict the freedom of black people in public spaces; they restricted the ability of black people to vote as well. The most common kinds of these voter suppression laws were:

- **poll taxes:** In order to cast a ballot, the voter had to pay a fee. Since black people were generally poorer than white people, this law hit them hardest. Some states created grandfather clauses that said if a person's grandfather hadn't paid a tax, they didn't have to either. This made it easier for poor white people to vote, but most black people's grandfathers hadn't legally been able to vote, so poll taxes remained a barrier specifically for black people.[4]

- **literacy tests:** If someone wanted to register to vote, they were required to pass a test first. The test could be a difficult quiz about the federal or state constitution, or it could be something as ridiculous as "How many bubbles are in a bar of soap?" State lawmakers claimed that literacy tests ensured that voters would be educated and informed. However, these tests were aimed at poor people, immigrants, and, in the South, black people. The administration of these tests was also unfair; the person in charge of registration could choose what questions to ask and how to grade the test, meaning nonwhite voters could be given more difficult questions or could receive failing grades even for correct answers.[5]

- **voter purges:** The state government could remove names from the official list of registered voters, which meant they couldn't vote on Election Day. White officials often took the names of black voters off the lists, and the voter wouldn't be informed until it was too late to register again for the election.[6]

- **disenfranchisement for moral turpitude:** Starting in 1894, states began passing laws that allowed them to take the right to vote away from anyone who committed even a minor crime. Black people were then targeted for arrest, sometimes under false charges—and a single arrest could lead to a person losing the right to vote forever.[7]

While these kinds of laws were typical of the Jim Crow South, similar laws were passed elsewhere in the United States. Northern states passed moral turpitude laws to deprive people of the right to vote. In 1894, California voters affirmed an education requirement that only allowed people who could read the US Constitution in English to vote, a measure meant to disenfranchise the state's Chinese population. Natives of China had already been excluded from voting in California in 1879. Washington required that voters be able to read and speak English starting in 1896. Oregon also passed a law in 1924 requiring that voters be able to read in English.[8]

When they weren't deterred by racist laws, nonwhite voters faced intimidation and violence from white people if they tried to exercise their rights. During Reconstruction, federal soldiers had acted to protect black voters. In 1878, Congress no longer allowed this, and by 1894, lawmakers had taken funding away from federal marshals who had also protected voters. Black people in the South were regularly threatened or subjected to violence and targeted by white supremacist organizations such as the Ku Klux Klan. Public officials and police generally either ignored the violence and threats or participated in them themselves.[9]

The Twenty-Fourth Amendment

Of all the voter suppression measures, the one that received the most national attention was poll taxes. During the election of 1938, Franklin D. Roosevelt relentlessly attacked poll taxes, recognizing that the ability of poor people of all colors to vote in the South was important to his policy agenda. His efforts to push for the abolition of poll taxes were ultimately unsuccessful.

Over the next twenty-five years, the issue came up in Congress several times and was defeated. President John F. Kennedy pushed not just to have Congress pass a law prohibiting poll taxes but to make it a constitutional amendment. This time, when a conservative Democrat from Florida introduced the amendment in the Senate, it passed. By January 23, 1964,

Redistricting

Most states are divided into a series of districts that group people in an area together. Districts are represented by state and local legislators and by members of the House of Representatives. Every ten years, after the census records how the US population has grown, shrunk, or shifted, districts are redrawn.

The Supreme Court decreed in the mid-1960s that districts had to hold roughly the same number of people, but how and where lines are drawn is left to the states. Sometimes, district boundaries are drawn in such a way that voters for one party or another are concentrated into a district, which is called gerrymandering. This can unfairly limit the legislators one party can have, creating an unbreakable majority for the other party.[10]

KEY VOTING LAWS

South Dakota became the thirty-eighth state to ratify it. Laws that stopped people from voting "by reason of failure to pay any poll tax or other tax" were now unconstitutional—at least in national elections.

By the time the Twenty-Fourth Amendment passed, only five states still had a poll tax: Alabama, Arkansas, Mississippi, Texas, and Virginia. Virginia, Alabama, and Texas ratified the amendment in the decades after it became law; Arkansas and Mississippi still have not.[11]

The Voting Rights Act of 1965

The oppression black people faced throughout the United States was not something they simply accepted. Ordinary people fought in the courts and protested in the streets in the decades that followed the end of Reconstruction. By the 1950s, the grassroots movements had reached a critical mass that we now call the civil rights movement.

The civil rights movement was a social war with many fronts. One important battle was the effort to end suppression of black voters. This was dangerous work for people in the movement; the Ku Klux Klan burned twenty black churches in Mississippi in the summer of 1964 alone. On June 21 of that summer, Michael Schwerner, James Chaney, and Andrew Goodman, three young men who had volunteered to help with voter registration efforts in Mississippi, were first arrested by

On March 7, 1965, people protesting the suppression of black voters were attacked by white law enforcement officers in Selma, Alabama.

KEY VOTING LAWS

local police and then murdered after they'd been released from custody.[12] On March 7, 1965, people protesting the suppression of black voters were attacked by white law enforcement officers on the Edmund Pettus Bridge in Selma, Alabama.

The brutality used on the Edmund Pettus Bridge made national news and was broadcast into living rooms across America. President Lyndon B. Johnson used the shock and revulsion so many Americans felt at the sight of the violence to break the opposition of Southern politicians in Congress and force the issue onto the floor. Congressional hearings showed that existing antidiscrimination laws weren't enough to stop voter suppression.[13]

As they drafted a new voting rights law, Congress decided that states with a history of voter suppression needed to have any laws that affected the vote approved by the Department of Justice before they could go into effect, which was called preclearance. The bill outlawed poll taxes in state and local elections and instructed the attorney general to sue states that used them. It also banned voting qualifications that targeted people on account of race, color, or language. It banned any test or device that interfered with voter registration or casting a ballot, such as literacy tests. It also said that states could not require someone to live in the state for more than thirty days before being able to register. Furthermore, the law prohibited people from falsely registering as a voter or voting twice.[14]

On August 6, 1965, President Johnson signed the Voting Rights Act with civil rights activists Martin Luther King Jr., Rosa Parks, and John Lewis standing behind him.

CHAPTER 5

What Do You Mean, They Couldn't Vote?

The story of the civil rights movement and the Voting Rights Act of 1965 might have already been familiar to you before reading this book. The Fourteenth, Fifteenth, and Nineteenth Amendments to the US Constitution all expanded voting rights immensely on paper, if not always in practice. The civil rights movement and the Voting Rights Act of 1965 helped to strengthen these rights. However, these major milestones are only part of the laws that have shaped the voting population into what you're familiar with today: generally any citizen over the age of eighteen.

The Indian Citizenship Act of 1924

Native Americans who lived on reservations were specifically excluded from United States citizenship when the Fourteenth Amendment was written in 1866. When the Fifteenth Amendment passed, it provided no protection for Native Americans because they weren't citizens.

KEY VOTING LAWS

When the Fifteenth Amendment passed, it provided no protection for Native Americans, who weren't considered citizens despite having lived in North America long before anyone who was considered a citizen.

In 1887, Congress passed the Dawes Act, which tried to coerce Native Americans to assimilate into the prevailing white culture by breaking up tribes and communal tribal lands and forcibly removing Native American children to special schools, where they could be indoctrinated. Part of why the Dawes Act was passed was the view at the time that if Native Americans were assimilated, then they could be given citizenship—and voting rights. Native Americans who accepted individual land allotments taken from their tribal lands and lived separately from their tribes were granted citizenship.

The effects of the Dawes Act were profoundly destructive to Native American people and allowed the government to sell much of their remaining land to white settlers at extremely low prices. The Burke Act amended the Dawes Act in 1906 so that Native Americans who accepted allotments were given citizenship without being required to separate from their tribe.

In 1924, the Indian Citizenship Act finally granted all Native Americans citizenship. However, it did nothing to enforce the voting rights of the new citizens; this was left to the states. Many states disenfranchised Native American citizens by denying them the right to vote because they lived on reservations or due to their tax status. In 1962, thirty-eight years later, New Mexico became the last state to comply with the Indian Citizenship Act when it changed its state constitution to remove a provision that had prevented Native Americans on reservations from voting. However, even today, Native Americans suffer from voter suppression efforts in certain states.[1]

The Magnuson Act

The Chinese Exclusion Act of 1882 stopped the immigration of Chinese laborers into the United States. This was the climax of growing American racism toward Chinese people. Chinese immigration had begun increasing during the California gold

KEY VOTING LAWS

How USA voted 2016

Democrats | Republicans

The winning Electoral Votes

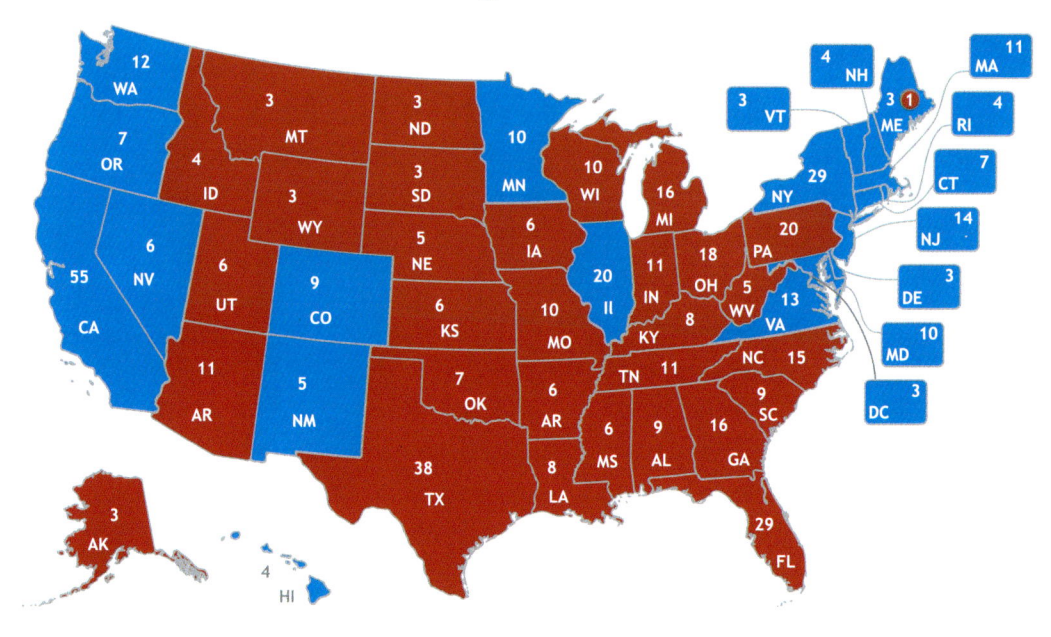

State	EV
WA	12
MT	3
ND	3
MN	10
NH	4
VT	3
ME	3 (1)
MA	11
RI	4
OR	7
ID	4
SD	3
WI	10
MI	16
NY	29
CT	7
NJ	14
CA	55
NV	6
UT	6
WY	3
NE	5
IA	6
IN	11
OH	18
PA	20
WV	5
VA	13
DE	3
MD	10
CO	9
KS	6
MO	10
KY	8
NC	15
DC	3
AZ	11
NM	5
OK	7
AR	6
TN	11
SC	9
TX	38
LA	8
MS	6
AL	9
GA	16
FL	29
AK	3
HI	4

Every state has a number of electoral votes that is based on its population. These votes are awarded to presidential candidates, and the candidate who gains the majority—at least 270—wins.

rush, and more Chinese laborers were brought in for large construction projects, such as the transcontinental railroad. The Exclusion Act barred Chinese immigrants from becoming American citizens as well.

The Magnuson Act of 1943 repealed the Chinese Exclusion Act, allowing Chinese people to finally become citizens. Theoretically, this meant they could vote, though they faced disenfranchisement measures such as poll taxes and literacy tests as well.

WHAT DO YOU MEAN, THEY COULDN'T VOTE?

The Magnuson Act also included a quota system to severely limit immigrants from China and certain other countries. The quota system was not abolished until the passage of the Immigration and Nationality Act of 1965.[2]

The Twenty-Third Amendment

Washington, DC, is not a state, so the people who live there are also technically not citizens of a state. They do not have voting representation in Congress because of this. In the 1970s, the city was granted a single delegate to the House of Representatives, but this delegate is not allowed to vote. Washington, DC, has a city council that its residents can vote for, but Congress has direct oversight, which means that it can overrule the decisions of the city council if it wishes.

In 1961, Congress passed the Twenty-Third Amendment, which allowed residents of Washington, DC, to vote in

Voting in US-Owned Territories

The United States has sixteen island territories scattered across the Pacific Ocean and Caribbean Sea. The five largest territories are Guam, the Northern Mariana Islands, Puerto Rico, the US Virgin Islands, and American Samoa. People who live in the first four are American citizens; people who live in American Samoa are American nationals. About 4 million people total live in these territories.

The citizens who live in the territories can vote in their local elections and presidential primaries, but they cannot vote in presidential elections. They also do not have representation in Congress; each territory gets only a nonvoting delegate.[3]

KEY VOTING LAWS

presidential elections. The amendment sets the number of electoral votes for Washington, DC, at three: equal to that of the least populous state.[4]

Currently, the least populous states in the United States are Wyoming, with a population of 577,737 as of 2018, and Vermont, with a population of 626,299 as of 2018. Meanwhile, Washington, DC, had a population of 702,455 in 2018.

The Twenty-Sixth Amendment

For most of America's history, the youngest age at which anyone could vote was twenty-one. Throughout America's history, soldiers far younger than that fought and died in our wars. The disconnect between who could die for America and who was allowed to vote for the politicians who decided if there would be wars was not lost on some lawmakers. After the US Civil War, delegates to New York's constitutional convention tried to lower the voting age to eighteen, though they were unsuccessful.

Decades later, President Dwight D. Eisenhower, who was a five-star general during World War II, mentioned the voting age in his second State of the Union address in 1954. He said, "For years, our citizens between the ages of eighteen and twenty-one have, in time of peril, been summoned to fight for America. They should participate in the political process that produces this fateful summons. I urge Congress to propose to the States a constitutional amendment permitting citizens to vote when they reach the age of eighteen."[5]

A decade later, America was embroiled in the Vietnam War and drafting soldiers, mostly from poor and working-class families. The war became increasingly unpopular, with widespread national protests beginning in 1965. Student activists in these protests resurrected a slogan from World War II: "Old enough to fight, old enough to vote."[6]

WHAT DO YOU MEAN, THEY COULDN'T VOTE?

In 1970, Senator Edward "Ted" Kennedy (*left*) debated with others about lowering the voting age, given that eighteen-year-old citizens were allowed to fight wars but not yet vote.

Congress attempted to lower the voting age to eighteen in 1970 when it voted to extend the Voting Rights Act. The Supreme Court ruled that while the federal government had the power to lower the voting age for federal elections, it couldn't force states to do so for state elections. There had to be a constitutional amendment.[7]

Worried about confusion in the next election, Congress moved quickly to propose the Twenty-Sixth Amendment in March 1971. Two months later, which is the quickest any amendment has been ratified, the Twenty-Sixth Amendment was entered into the Constitution. Instantly, 11 million citizens gained the vote.[8]

CHAPTER 6

Voting in Modern America

In theory, every United States citizen over the age of eighteen should be able to vote. However, as in the Jim Crow era, when black citizens should have been able to vote but were blocked by a variety of laws, the reality is much more complicated—and unfair. Felons are not the only ones who are denied the right to vote in many states.

The National Voter Registration Act of 1993

While the Voting Rights Act of 1965 abolished many state practices that made registering and voting more difficult, there were no national standards on voter registration. After passing the Voting Rights Act, Congress attempted to address this issue and standardize voter registration, but no measures passed. In the late 1980s, Congress came up with the idea of directing state motor vehicle agencies to offer people the chance to register to vote when they got their driver's license or state ID. In 1993, that idea finally became a law with the National Voter Registration Act, also known as the Motor Voter Act.

VOTING IN MODERN AMERICA

In 1993, President Bill Clinton signed the Motor Voter Act into law, ensuring that people could register to vote at every DMV location while obtaining or renewing a driver's license or state ID.

The Motor Voter Act requires state agencies to offer eligible people the opportunity to register to vote when they get an ID or register for public assistance. It also says that the US Postal Service must mail election materials for states. States are exempted from the act if they offer voter registration on Election Day itself or don't require people to be registered in order to vote.[1]

Shelby County v. Holder

Shelby County, Alabama, filed a court case in Washington, DC, challenging Section 5 of the Voting Rights Act in April 2010. Section 5 was the part of the Voting Rights Act that required

49

KEY VOTING LAWS

preclearance of election laws from states that had a history of racist voter suppression—such as Alabama. The US district court in Washington, DC, upheld the constitutionality of Section 5 in September 2011. A US court of appeals agreed with the district court in May of 2012.

Shelby County appealed the case to the Supreme Court. The court did not declare Section 5 unconstitutional, but in a 5–4 decision on June 25, 2013, it ruled that part of Section 4 was. This part of Section 4 was what determined which areas required preclearance; the majority of the court said that the data used to make this determination was more than forty years old and didn't reflect current needs. This effectively ended preclearance because without that part of Section 4, there were no longer any jurisdictions listed that required preclearance.

In her dissenting opinion, Justice Ruth Bader Ginsburg wrote that "throwing out preclearance when it had worked and is continuing to work to stop discriminatory changes is like throwing away your umbrella in a rainstorm because you are not getting wet."[2]

The Commission on Civil Rights issued a report in 2018 stating that at least twenty-three states had enacted "newly restrictive statewide voter laws" since the 2013 Supreme Court decision in *Shelby County v. Holder*. These laws and other state actions included closing polling places, purging voter rolls, cutting early voting days, and enacting new voter ID laws. While more than sixty lawsuits had been filed challenging these new, restrictive laws as of 2018, most of those lawsuits did not come from the Department of Justice (DOJ), which used to be in charge of preclearance. Four were filed by the DOJ during the Obama administration, though none were filed by the DOJ under Trump.

Catherine Lhamon, chair of the Commission on Civil Rights, said that citizens in these states "continue to suffer significant, and profoundly unequal, limitations on their right to vote."[3]

Voter ID Laws

As of 2019, thirty-five states request or require that voters show some form of identification in order to vote. Ten of these states (Georgia, Indiana, Kansas, Mississippi, Tennessee, Virginia, Wisconsin, Arizona, North Dakota, and Ohio) have what the National Conference of State Legislatures characterizes as strict requirements, meaning that people without the required ID can only cast provisional ballots and have to take action like going to the election office a few days after the election to show the right ID if they want their ballot to be counted. Some states will accept several different forms of identification, including nonphoto ID, while others require much more specific IDs.[4]

As of 2019, thirty-five states request or require some form of identification in order to vote. Strict ID requirements can make it difficult or impossible for some people to vote.

KEY VOTING LAWS

A major criticism of voter ID laws is that strict ID requirements can make it difficult or impossible for some people to get the required ID, particularly elderly people and people of color. This is because some people may not have the exact documentation required. Research done by the *Washington Post* shows that voter ID laws suppress voting by people of color.[5]

In one example, a ninety-six-year-old black woman who had voted during the Jim Crow era later applied for the ID required by Tennessee and was denied because the last name on her birth certificate didn't match her married name and she didn't have a copy of her marriage license.[6] In 2018, the Supreme Court allowed a North Dakota law to change voter ID requirements so that people could not use a PO box for their address. Many Native Americans who live on reservations use PO boxes to register to vote.[7] These kinds of address requirements can also prevent homeless people from being able to vote.

Proponents of voter ID laws often say that strict ID prevents fraudulent voting, but multiple studies have shown that in-person voter fraud is extremely rare. Two studies from Arizona State University showed only ten cases of voter fraud between 2000 and 2012 in the entire United States.[8]

Exact Match

Brian Kemp became the governor of Georgia in a highly contested 2018 election. While he was running for governor, he was the secretary of state for Georgia, which meant he was in charge of the voter rolls and policies around voter registration.

A controversial policy he put into place as secretary of state in 2013 was called "exact match." This means that when someone registers to vote, the information on their application must exactly match state records, including punctuation and even spaces. Between 2013 and 2016, Georgia denied 36,874 voter registrations due to the policy. A lawsuit filed against

VOTING IN MODERN AMERICA

Brian Kemp won a highly contested election in Georgia in 2018 after establishing an "exact match" law when it came to voter registration.

KEY VOTING LAWS

Polling Place Problems

States decide where polling places will be and how many there will be. Sometimes polling places are closed because there aren't enough people around who need to use them. Other times, closed polling locations can lead to confusion and long lines. Maricopa County in Arizona closed 70 percent of its polling locations in the years after *Shelby County v. Holder*, causing five-hour waits at some locations.

In 2018, the polling place for Dodge City, Kansas, which has a large Latinx population, was moved outside the city limits and 1 mile (1.6 kilometers) from the nearest bus stop. Newly registered voters were given the address for the old location in their registration notification.[9]

the exact-match policy stated that black applicants were eight times more likely than white applicants to fail an exact match, while Asian American and Latinx applicants were six times more likely to fail than white applicants.

The lawsuit forced Kemp to suspend the policy in 2016 before the election, but in 2017, the Georgia legislature made exact match the law of the state. Other states, such as Florida, have an exact-match requirement for registration as well—but unlike in Georgia, these states require election officials to reconcile the difference. The Georgia law also does not have any quality-control requirements to identify problems with data entry. Supporters of the law in Georgia say it prevents fraudulent voting.[10] However, opponents say clerical errors that occur while trying to verify an exact match unnecessarily prevent people—especially people of color—from voting legally.

CHAPTER 7

What Is the Future of the Vote?

On March 8, 2019, the Democrat-controlled House of Representatives passed a bill called HR 1, also known as the For the People Act. Along with anticorruption and campaign finance measures, HR 1 included many voting and election reforms, such as declaring Election Day a federal holiday. While HR 1 had no chance of becoming law after the leader of the Senate, Republican Mitch McConnell, said he would not allow it to be voted on, it may be viewed as a wish list of measures that could be enacted in the future to make voting more accessible to all citizens.

Republicans have criticized HR 1 as overreach by the federal government. Other opponents have spread untrue rumors about it, such as claiming that it would allow undocumented immigrants to vote.[1] Much of American history has been a tug-of-war between expanding the idea of who can vote and finding ways to restrict who is allowed to actually cast a ballot. History has provided many examples of how voting can be restricted, but the state of Florida's passage of Amendment Four has provided a recent example of how voting restrictions can be undone.

How else could voting expand in the future?

KEY VOTING LAWS

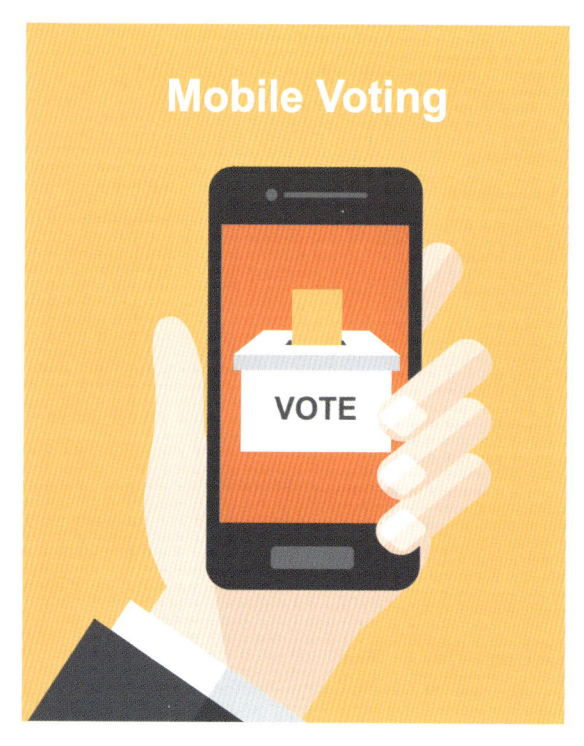

Mobile Voting

What will the future mean for voting? Some states already allow voting through the mail. Will we one day vote via mobile devices?

Automatic Voter Registration

What if, instead of having to fill out an application to register to vote, it happened automatically when you turned eighteen? As of 2019, sixteen states and Washington, DC, have laws that automatically register citizens to vote unless they opt out of it. In some states, people can opt out when they are notified by the state that they have been registered. In other states, they can opt out while interacting with a state agency, such as when they're renewing their ID or driver's license. Voters can choose which political party they want to be affiliated with; if they do not choose, they are marked as unaffiliated.

A benefit of automatic voter registration is that it makes it easier for people to vote and means there is no longer a possibility that someone will miss out on an election by not turning the registration form in on time. It also helps maintain voter rolls because voting information gets automatically updated every time the voter interacts with the state government. Opponents of automatic voter registration point out concerns about data privacy. Some consider it an infringement of the right to free speech or believe that it will lead to voter fraud because noncitizens can legally obtain state IDs.[2]

Election Day as a National Holiday

A recent Pew Research poll showed 65 percent of Americans would like Election Day, which is always held on a Tuesday, to be a national holiday. Making Election Day a national holiday would make voting easier. Many people would automatically have the day off from work, and a poll of nonvoters showed that scheduling issues and difficulty reaching a polling place were major reasons why they did not vote.

Most states allow voters to take time off of work to vote, but there is no federal law for that. Since many people, such as service workers and emergency workers, have to be at their jobs even on federal holidays, it is unknown how a holiday would affect voting for them.[3]

Nonpartisan Redistricting

Generally, for a representative democracy, you would expect to have half of the seats if you win half of the vote. However, the way congressional districts were drawn had a major effect in the Congressional election of 2018. For example, in North Carolina, Republicans got 51 percent of the vote in the state but won ten (77 percent) of the state's thirteen seats in the House of Representatives. In contrast, Pennsylvania was forced by court order to redraw its gerrymandered maps before the election. In Pennsylvania in 2018, Democrats won 54 percent of the vote, which gave them and the Republicans each nine seats.[4]

States with unfairly drawn districts that favor a major party are often taken to court. In 2019, cases from North Carolina and Maryland were appealed to the Supreme Court because of gerrymandering by Republicans and Democrats, respectively.

KEY VOTING LAWS

Representatives and legislators are elected from districts, which should be divided evenly among voters, but gerrymandering—a practice with the intent to disenfranchise groups of people—makes those divisions unfair.

Lower courts had ordered the states to redraw their maps more fairly. However, the Supreme Court ruled in *Rucho v. Common Cause* that it was not the responsibility of the judicial branch to prevent partisan gerrymandering, allowing the maps to stand.[5]

In 2018, voters in Michigan, Utah, Missouri, Colorado, and Ohio decided they wanted redistricting to be nonpartisan in some way, such as making committees an even split between political parties or selecting committees of nonpoliticians to decide. These developments in traditionally conservative states such as Utah as well as traditionally liberal states such as Colorado show that voters across the political spectrum have an interest in elections being fair. There are currently efforts underway in Arkansas, Oklahoma, and Virginia to make redistricting nonpartisan before the 2020 census, which will cause districts to be redrawn in 2021.[6]

Vote by Mail

Colorado, Washington, and Oregon conduct all of their elections using mail-in ballots. Voters receive ballots in the mail several weeks before the election, and then they may either mail them back or drop them off at a ballot box. Nineteen other states have laws that allow some elections to be conducted by mail.

Elections with mail-in ballots tend to be more convenient for voters, letting them fill out ballots when it's convenient for them and turn them in at the mailbox. It also makes elections

How Secure Is Your Vote?

Voting through the internet is one possible future, but it is one that comes with security concerns—what if hackers intercept and change votes? However, hacking is already a threat. Before the election of 2016, Russian hackers successfully attacked the email servers of the Democratic Party. Hackers also breached the Illinois Board of Elections.

In 2016, the Department of Homeland Security recommended security practices such as patching software and making sure that vote-counting machines were not on the internet at all. However, security experts caution that electronic voting machines can be hacked. Some machines do not provide paper receipts, and many states do not do manual audits to check electronic machines. Hackers could also potentially alter voter databases.[7]

KEY VOTING LAWS

More than twenty states have laws that allow mail-in ballots in at least some circumstances. Colorado, Oregon, and Washington conduct all of their elections by mail, including presidential elections.

more accessible for people who may be housebound or have reasons they cannot easily go to a polling place on Election Day. The convenience factor may help turnout in elections that are conducted by mail. The US Postal Service delivers all mailed ballots whether they include proper postage or not.

Elections conducted entirely by mail may be less useful in some areas, such as reservations, where residents may not have standard street addresses or share post office boxes.[8]

Ranked-Choice Voting

Ranked-choice voting is a system that may be unfamiliar to people in the United States, though it has been in use in

Australia since 1918. Fourteen other countries use some sort of ranked-choice voting as well. There are several subtypes of ranked-choice voting, but the basics of the system are that a voter can choose multiple candidates to vote for and put them in order of preference. This means the candidate the voter wants most will be ranked "1," the candidate the voter wants second most will be "2," and so on.

In ranked-choice voting, you can leave candidates you do not want to vote for at all blank or only vote for one person. If your first choice cannot win because he or she has received too few votes, then your vote goes to your second choice, and so on. One argument for ranked-choice voting is that it may give smaller political parties a greater chance at having their candidates elected because voters will be less worried about potentially wasting their vote on a minor-party candidate. Opponents point out that it can be a complicated and confusing system.

There are several cities in the United States that use some form of ranked-choice voting in their municipal elections. Maine became the first state in America to use the system in a federal election in 2018. Democrat Jared Golden defeated Republican incumbent Bruce Poliquin in the election for a House seat; Poliquin demanded a recount and challenged the constitutionality of ranked-choice voting in court after the result of the vote was declared.[9] The court ruled against Poliquin, pointing out that the US Constitution allows states to decide how they will conduct elections.[10]

In the wake of the 2018 election, a bill for ranked-choice voting was introduced in Vermont. The voting system has become a topic for discussion in other states and more cities.

All of these ideas about the future of voting are already being run as experiments in America and around the world. What else might the future hold to make voting easier—or more restrictive?

CHRONOLOGY

1619 The first representative assembly in colonial America meets on July 30 in Jamestown, Virginia.

1775 The American Revolutionary War begins on April 19 with "the shot heard round the world."

1777 The Articles of Confederation are sent to the states. The government they outline leaves the administration of elections and the vote to the discretion of the states.

1783 The American Revolutionary War ends.

1787 The Constitutional Convention begins to draft the Constitution of the United States of America, which goes into effect two years later on March 4, 1789.

1790 The Naturalization Act of 1790 indicates that white male immigrants can become citizens after living in the United States for two years. As time passes, the definition of who can become a citizen changes and expands.

1848 The Seneca Falls Convention begins on July 19.

1856 North Carolina becomes the last state to eliminate property requirements for voting.

1861 The US Civil War begins with the attack on Fort Sumter on April 12.

1865 The US Civil War ends on April 9, and the Thirteenth Amendment to the Constitution is ratified by the states on December 6.

1868 The Fourteenth Amendment becomes law on July 9, declaring that all people born in the United States are citizens and that eligible male citizens cannot be denied the right to vote.

1870 The Fifteenth Amendment becomes law on March 30, theoretically guaranteeing the voting rights of black men. The lack of inclusion of women in the amendment causes a serious schism in the women's suffrage movement.

CHRONOLOGY

1896 *Plessy v. Ferguson* is decided, codifying "separate but equal" and paving the way for Jim Crow laws in the South, some of which are used to disenfranchise black voters.

1914 World War I begins on July 28, though the United States does not enter the war until April 6, 1917.

1918 World War I ends on November 11. By now, twenty states and territories have given women the right to vote.

1920 The Nineteenth Amendment is ratified on August 18, granting women the right to vote. On November 2, 8 million women vote in elections across the country for the first time.

1924 The Indian Citizenship Act grants citizenship to all Native Americans. Thirty-eight years later, New Mexico becomes the final state to comply with its provisions, though Native Americans suffer from voter suppression efforts even today.

1939 World War II begins on September 1, though the United States does not formally enter the war until after the attack on Pearl Harbor on December 7, 1941.

1945 World War II ends on September 2.

1954 Chief Justice Earl Warren writes in *Brown v. Board of Education of Topeka,* "Separate educational facilities are inherently unequal," signaling the beginning of the end for Jim Crow laws.

1955 The Montgomery bus boycott begins on December 5 to protest segregated seating. The boycott lasts 381 days. The Vietnam War begins on November 1.

1961 The Twenty-Third Amendment gives residents of Washington, DC, the right to vote in presidential elections.

1963 On August 28, more than 200,000 people participate in the March on Washington to protest racial discrimination.

1964 Poll taxes for federal elections are made unconstitutional by the ratification of the Twenty-Fourth Amendment on January 23.

KEY VOTING LAWS

1965 The Voting Right Act is signed into law on August 6, outlawing many barriers to voting and placing states with a history of racist voter suppression under the requirement of preclearance.

1971 The Twenty-Sixth Amendment lowers the voting age to eighteen, driven in part by anti–Vietnam War protests by student activists under the banner of "Old enough to fight, old enough to vote."

1973 The Vietnam War ends on January 27 with the fall of Saigon.

1993 The National Voter Registration Act of 1993, also called the Motor Voter Act, requires states across the country to offer people the opportunity to register to vote when they get their driver's license or state ID.

2013 *Shelby County v. Holder* ends the Voting Rights Act preclearance requirement in a 5–4 Supreme Court decision. In the next five years, twenty-three states enact newly restrictive voter laws.

2019 In Florida, 1.5 million people are able to register to vote on January 8, thanks to the passage of Amendment Four ending felony disenfranchisement. On March 8, the Democrat-controlled House of Representatives passes HR 1, proposing sweeping election reforms that would make voting easier. In June, the Supreme Court decides *Rucho v. Common Cause*, refusing to get involved in partisan gerrymanding in North Carolina and Maryland.

CHAPTER NOTES

Introduction

1. "Florida's Ex-Felon Voting Rules Slow to Impact Registration," NBC News, February 24, 2019, www.nbcnews.com/politics/meet-the-press/florida-s-ex-felon-voting-rules-slow-impact-registration-n975041 (accessed March 15, 2019).
2. "Felony Disenfranchisement Laws (Map)," ACLU.org, accessed on March 1, 2019, www.aclu.org/issues/voting-rights/voter-restoration/felony-disenfranchisement-laws-map.
3. "The Racist Origins of Felon Disenfranchisement," *New York Times*, November 18, 2014, www.nytimes.com/2014/11/19/opinion/the-racist-origins-of-felon-disenfranchisement.html.
4. "Desmond Meade Helps Restore Voting Rights to Millions of Ex-Felons Across Florida," *Orlando Sentinel*, February 5, 2019, www.orlandosentinel.com/opinion/central-floridian-of-the-year/os-ae-desmond-meade-ex-felon-voting-rights-20190130-story.html.

CHAPTER 1: Foundational Voting Laws

1. "Athens," British Museum, accessed on March 4, 2019, www.ancientgreece.co.uk/athens/home_set.html.
2. "Election," *Encyclopedia Britannica*, accessed on March 4, 2019, www.britannica.com/topic/election-political-science.
3. "A Brief Chronology of the House of Commons," Parliament.uk, accessed on March 15, 2019, www.parliament.uk/documents/commons-information-office/g03.pdf.
4. "Voting in Early America," Colonial Williamsburg, accessed on March 4, 2019, www.history.org/foundation/journal/spring07/elections.cfm.
5. "Magna Carta: Muse and Mentor," Library of Congress, accessed on March 15, 2019, www.loc.gov/exhibits/magna-carta-muse-and-mentor/no-taxation-without-representation.html.

6. "Articles of Confederation," *Encyclopedia Britannica*, accessed on March 15, 2019, www.britannica.com/topic/Articles-of-Confederation.
7. "Articles of Confederation 1777–1781," Office of the Historian, accessed on March 15, 2019, history.state.gov/milestones/1776-1783/articles.
8. "State Houses Elect Senators," United States Senate, accessed on March 15, 2019, www.senate.gov/artandhistory/history/minute/State_Houses_Elect_Senators.htm.
9. "James Madison, Note to His Speech on the Right to Suffrage," Founder's Constitution, accessed on March 15, 2019, press-pubs.uchicago.edu/founders/documents/v1ch16s26.html.
10. "The Constitution of the United States: A Transcription," National Archives, accessed on March 15, 2019, www.archives.gov/founding-docs/constitution-transcript.
11. "Expansion of Rights and Liberties—The Right of Suffrage," Charters of Freedom, accessed on March 15, 2019, web.archive.org/web/20160706144856/http://www.archives.gov/exhibits/charters/charters_of_freedom_13.html.
12. "Women's Rights After the American Revolution," Women History Blog, accessed on March 15, 2019, www.womenhistoryblog.com/2013/06/womens-rights-after-american-revolution.html.
13. "For a Few Decades in the 18th Century, Women and African-Americans Could Vote in New Jersey," *Smithsonian*, November 16, 2017, www.smithsonianmag.com/smart-news/why-black-people-and-women-lost-vote-new-jersey-180967186/.
15. Eric Ledell Smith, "The End of Black Voting Rights in Pennsylvania: African Americans and the Pennsylvania Constitutional Convention of 1837–1838," *Pennsylvania History: A Journal of Mid-Atlantic Studies*, vol. 65, no. 3 (Summer 1998).
16. "Non-Citizens Used to Be Able to Vote in U. S. Electons. Here's What Changed," *Time*, July 18, 2017, time.com/4859478/immigrant-voters-history.

17. 1 Stat. 103.

Chapter 2: (Almost) Universal Male Suffrage

1. "The Evolution of Suffrage Institutions in the New World," Yale, February 2005, economics.yale.edu/sites/default/files/files/Workshops-Seminars/Economic-History/sokoloff-050406.pdf.
2. "The Declaration of Causes of Seceding States," American Battlefield Trust, accessed on March 15, 2019, www.battlefields.org/learn/primary-sources/declaration-causes-seceding-states.
3. "13th Amendment to the Constitution of the United States," Smithsonian—National Museum of African American History and Culture, accessed on March 15, 2019, nmaahc.si.edu/blog-post/13th-amendment-constitution-united-states.
4. "After 148 Years, Mississippi Finally Ratifies 13th Amendment, Which Banned Slavery," CBS, February 18, 2013, www.cbsnews.com/news/after-148-years-mississippi-finally-ratifies-13th-amendment-which-banned-slavery/.
5. "Race and Voting in the Segregated South," Constitutional Rights Foundation, accessed on March 15, 2019, www.crf-usa.org/black-history-month/race-and-voting-in-the-segregated-south.
6. W. E. B. Du Bois, *Black Reconstruction in America: An Essay Toward a History of the Part Which Black Folk Played in the Attempt to Reconstruct Democracy in America, 1860-1880* (Oxford, UK: Oxford University Press, 1935), pp. 151–323.
7. "14th Amendment," History.com, accessed on March 15, 2019, www.history.com/topics/black-history/fourteenth-amendment.
8. William Gillette, "Fifteenth Amendment (Framing and Ratification)," *Encyclopedia of the American Constitution*, 2nd ed. (New York: MacMillan Reference, 2000), pp. 1039–1041.

KEY VOTING LAWS

Chapter 3: Women Win the Right to Vote

1. "Letter from Abigail Adams to John Adams, 31 March—5 April 1776," Massachusetts Historical Society, accessed on March 15, 2019, www.masshist.org/digitaladams/archive/doc?id=L17760331aa.
2. "Elizabeth Cady Stanton," National Women's History Museum, accessed on March 15, 2019, www.womenshistory.org/education-resources/biographies/elizabeth-cady-stanton.
3. "History of Woman Suffrage," Uncle Tom's Cabin & American Culture, accessed on March 15, 2019, utc.iath.virginia.edu/abolitn/abwmat.html.
4. "How the Suffrage Movement Betrayed Black Women," *New York Times,* July 28, 2018, www.nytimes.com/2018/07/28/opinion/sunday/suffrage-movement-racism-black-women.html.
5. "14th and 15th Amendment," National Women's History Museum, accessed on March 15, 2019, www.crusadeforthevote.org/14-15-amendments.
6. "(1888) Frederick Douglass on Woman Suffrage," Black Past, accessed on March 15, 2019, blackpast.org/1888-frederick-douglass-woman-suffrage.
7. "In America; Stanton and Anthony," *New York Times*, July 4, 1999, www.nytimes.com/1999/07/04/opinion/in-america-stanton-and-anthony.html.
8. "Women's Suffrage Leaders Left Out Black Women," *Teen Vogue,* August 18, 2017, www.teenvogue.com/story/womens-suffrage-leaders-left-out-black-women.
9. "17th Amendment to the U.S. Constitution: Direct Election of U.S. Senators," National Archives, accessed on March 15, 2019, www.archives.gov/legislative/features/17th-amendment.
10. "19th Amendment," History.com, accessed on March 15, 2019, www.history.com/topics/womens-history/19th-amendment-1.

CHAPTER NOTES

11. "Abolition, Women's Rights, and Temperance Movements," NPS, accessed on March 15, 2019, www.nps.gov/wori/learn/historyculture/abolition-womens-rights-and-temperance-movements.htm.
12. "'Durable White Supremacy': Belle Kearney Puts Black Men in Their Place," History Matters, U.S. Survey Course on the Web, accessed on March 15, 2019, historymatters.gmu.edu/d/5317.
13. "The Original Women's March on Washington and the Suffragists Who Paved the Way," *Smithsonian*, January 21, 2017, www.smithsonianmag.com/history/original-womens-march-washington-and-suffragists-who-paved-way-180961869.
14. "Woodrow Wilson and the Women's Suffrage Movement: A Reflection," Wilson Center, accessed on March 15, 2019, www.wilsoncenter.org/article/woodrow-wilson-and-the-womens-suffrage-movement-reflection.
15. "Women's Suffrage: Tennessee and the Passage of the 19th Amendment," Tennessee Secretary of State, accessed on March 15, 2019, sos.tn.gov/products/tsla/womens-suffrage-tennessee-and-passage-19th-amendment.

CHAPTER 4: Voter Suppression

1. "Jim Crow Law," *Encyclopedia Britannica*, accessed on March 15, 2019, www.britannica.com/event/Jim-Crow-law.
2. *Homer A. Plessy v. John H. Ferguson*, 163 U.S. 537 (1896).
3. *Brown v. Board of Education*, 374 U.S. 483 (1954).
4. "Poll Taxes," Smithsonian National Museum of American History, accessed on March 15, 2019, americanhistory.si.edu/democracy-exhibition/vote-voice/keeping-vote/state-rules-federal-rules/poll-taxes.
5. "Literacy Tests," Smithsonian National Museum of American History, accessed on March 15, 2019, americanhistory.si.edu/democracy-exhibition/vote-voice/keeping-vote/state-rules-federal-rules/literacy-tests.

KEY VOTING LAWS

6. "Voting Rights for Blacks and Poor Whites in the Jim Crow South," America's Black Holocaust Museum, accessed on March 15, 2019, abhmuseum.org/voting-rights-for-blacks-and-poor-whites-in-the-jim-crow-south.
7. "The Racist Origins of Felon Disenfranchisement," *New York Times*.
8. James Thomas Tucker, *The Battle Over Bilingual Ballots: Language Minorities and Political Access Under the Voting Rights Act* (New York: Routledge, 2016), pp. 6–22.
9. Bruce Ackerman and Jennifer Nou, "Canonizing the Civil Rights Revolution: The People and the Poll Tax," *Northwestern University Law Review*, vol. 103, no. 1 (2009).
10. "Redistricting," Brennan Center for Change, accessed on March 11, 2019, www.brennancenter.org/issues/redistricting.
11. "The Rise and Fall of Jim Crow: Jim Crow Stories," thirteen.org, accessed on March 15, 2019, www.thirteen.org/wnet/jimcrow/stories_org_kkk.html.
12. "Murder in Mississippi," PBS, accessed on March 15, 2019, www.pbs.org/wgbh/americanexperience/features/freedomsummer-murder.
13. "Voting Rights Act of 1965," Martin Luther King Jr. Research and Education Institute at Stanford, accessed on March 15, 2019, kinginstitute.stanford.edu/encyclopedia/voting-rights-act-1965.
14. 79 Stat. 437.

CHAPTER 5: What Do You Mean, They Couldn't Vote?

1. "Voting Rights for Native Americans," Library of Congress, accessed on March 11, 2019, www.loc.gov/teachers/classroommaterials/presentationsandactivities/presentations/elections/voting-rights-native-americans.html.

CHAPTER NOTES

2. "Repeal of the Chinese Exclusion Act, 1943," Office of the Historian, accessed on March 11, 2019, history.state.gov/milestones/1937-1945/chinese-exclusion-act-repeal.
3. "U.S. Territories," U.S. Citizenship and Immigration Services, accessed on March 11, 2019, www.uscis.gov/tools/glossary/us-territories.
4. "Twenty-Third Amendment," *Encyclopedia Britannica*, accessed on March 11, 2019, www.britannica.com/topic/Twenty-third-Amendment.
5. "Eisenhower's State of the Union Address, 1954," PBS, accessed on March 11, 2019, www.pbs.org/wgbh/americanexperience/features/eisenhower-state54.
6. "Records of Rights Vote: 'Old Enough to Fight, Old Enough to Vote,'" National Archives, accessed on March 15, 2019, prologue.blogs.archives.gov/2013/11/13/records-of-rights-vote-old-enough-to-fight-old-enough-to-vote.
7. "Supreme Court Partially Upholds Voting Rights for 18-Year-Olds, Dec. 21, 1970," Politico, December 21, 2017, www.politico.com/story/2017/12/21/this-day-in-politics-dec-21-1970-301739.
8. "The 26th Amendment," History.com, accessed on March 11, 2019, www.history.com/topics/united-states-constitution/the-26th-amendment.

CHAPTER 6: Voting in Modern America

1. 107 Stat. 77.
2. *Shelby County, Alabama v. Eric Holder, Jr., Attorney General, et al.*, 570 U.S. 529 (2013).
3. "Discriminatory Voter Laws Have Surged in Last 5 Years, Federal Commission Finds," CNN, September 12, 2018, edition.cnn.com/2018/09/12/politics/voting-rights-federal-commission-election/index.html.

4. "Voter Identification Requirements: Voter ID Laws," National Conference of State Legislatures, accessed on March 11, 2019, www.ncsl.org/research/elections-and-campaigns/voter-id.aspx.
5. "Getting a Photo ID So You Can Vote Is Easy. Unless You're Poor, Black, Latino, or Elderly," *Washington Post*, May 23, 2016, www.washingtonpost.com/politics/courts_law/getting-a-photo-id-so-you-can-vote-is-easy-unless-youre-poor-black-latino-or-elderly/2016/05/23/8d5474ec-20f0-11e6-8690-f14ca9de2972_story.html.
6. "96-Year-Old Woman Who Voted During Jim Crow Is Denied Photo ID," *Nashville Scene*, October 5, 2011, www.nashvillescene.com/news/pith-in-the-wind/article/13040146/96yearold-woman-who-voted-during-jim-crow-is-denied-photo-id.
7. "In Senate Battleground, Native American Voting Rights Activists Fight Back Against Voter ID Restrictions," *Washington Post*, October 12, 2018, www.washingtonpost.com/politics/in-senate-battleground-native-american-voting-rights-activists-fight-back-against-voter-id-restrictions/2018/10/12/7bc33ad2-cd60-11e8-a360-85875bac0b1f_story.html.
8. "Debunking the Voter Fraud Myth," Brennan Center for Justice, accessed on March 15, 2019, www.brennancenter.org/analysis/debunking-voter-fraud-myth.
9. "New Voters Get Notices Listing Wrong Dodge City Polling Site," Associated Press, October 25, 2018, www.apnews.com/e1b4e441d4a448b98f129fcde0556a98.
10. "Georgia's 'Exact Match' Law and the Abrams-Kemp Governor's Election, Explained," PolitiFact, October 19, 2018, www.politifact.com/georgia/article/2018/oct/19/georgias-exact-match-law-and-its-impact-voters-gov.

CHAPTER NOTES

CHAPTER 7: What Is the Future of the Vote?

1. "House Democrats Just Passed a Slate of Significant Reforms to Get Money Out of Politics," *Vox*, March 8, 2019, www.vox.com/2019/3/8/18253609/hr-1-pelosi-house-democrats-anti-corruption-mcconnell.
2. "Automatic Voter Registration," National Conference of State Legislatures, accessed on March 14, 2019, www.ncsl.org/research/elections-and-campaigns/automatic-voter-registration.aspx.
3. "Democrats Want to Make Election Day a National Holiday—Here's Why," CNBC, February 5, 2019, www.cnbc.com/2019/02/05/democrats-want-to-make-election-day-a-national-holidayheres-why.html.
4. "Election Shows How Gerrymandering Is Difficult to Overcome," *U.S. News & World Report*, November 17, 2018, www.usnews.com/news/politics/articles/2018-11-17/midterm-elections-reveal-effects-of-gerrymandered-districts.
5. "Supreme Court to Hear Cases on Partisan Gerrymandering," *Washington Post*, January 4, 2019, www.washingtonpost.com/politics/courts_law/supreme-court-to-hear-cases-on-partisan-gerrymandering/2019/01/04/6bd3ae46-0f8b-11e9-84fc-d58c33d6c8c7_story.html; and "Supreme Court Rules Partisan Gerrymandering Is Beyond the Reach of Federal Courts," NPR, June 27, 2019, www.npr.org/2019/06/27/731847977/supreme-court-rules-partisan-gerrymandering-is-beyond-the-reach-of-federal-court.
6. "Citizen and Legislative Efforts to Reform Redistricting in 2018," Brennan Center for Justice, accessed on March 15, 2019, www.brennancenter.org/analysis/current-citizen-efforts-reform-redistricting.
7. "The Crisis of Election Security," *New York Times*, September 26, 2018, www.nytimes.com/2018/09/26/magazine/election-security-crisis-midterms.html.

8. "All-Mail Elections (AKA Vote-by-Mail)," National Conference of State Legislatures, accessed March on 15, 2019, www.ncsl.org/research/elections-and-campaigns/all-mail-elections.aspx.
9. "The Somewhat Absurd Controversy Over Maine's Ranked Choice Voting System, Explained," *Vox*, December 9, 2018, www.vox.com/2018/12/9/18133184/maine-ranked-choice-voting-australia-ireland.
10. "Judge Rules Out New Election for Poliquin in Decision Upholding Maine's Ranked-Choice Voting," *Portland Press Herald*, December 13, 2018, www.pressherald.com/2018/12/13/federal-judge-rejects-poliquins-constitutional-challenge-of-ranked-choice-voting.

GLOSSARY

disenfranchisement The state of being denied a right or privilege, especially the right to vote.

disproportionate When the effect of something is too big or small compared to the size of the population. For example, 30 percent of the people who live in a state are nonwhite; the state makes a voter ID law and 70 percent of the people it prevents from voting are nonwhite. Therefore, the law disproportionately affects people of color.

franchise The right to vote.

gerrymandering Manipulating the boundaries of a political district to favor one party over another.

indoctrinate To teach people to accept a set of beliefs uncritically, sometimes involving force, coercion, or isolation from contradictory information.

inextricably In a way that is impossible to separate or disentangle.

lame duck session The period between an election and the end of the term; it is often used to indicate that an elected official is ineffectual or powerless because they are just waiting to leave office, but can mean they feel they can act without consequences because the election results have been decided.

municipal Relating to a city or town.

nonpartisan Not favoring or run by a particular political group. Often used interchangeably with "nonbiased," though the two are not necessarily the same.

recalcitrant Reluctant, uncooperative, or obstinate.

schism A split between two parts of the same group, caused by a strong disagreement.

segregation The separation of groups based on a characteristic such as race.

suffrage The right to vote.

unaffiliated Not belonging to any political party.

FURTHER READING

BOOKS

Anderson, Carol. *One Person, No Vote: How Voter Suppression Is Destroying Our Democracy.* New York, NY: Bloomsbury Publishing, 2018.

Barcella, Laura. *Know Your Rights! A Modern Kid's Guide to the American Constitution.* New York, NY: Sterling Children's Books, 2018.

Elish, Dan. *The Civil Rights Movement: Then and Now.* North Mankato, MN: Capstone Press, 2018.

Roosevelt, Eleanor, and Michelle Markel. *When You Grow Up to Vote: How Our Government Works for You.* New York, NY: Roaring Brook Press, 2018.

WEBSITES

Brennan Center for Justice
brennancenter.org
This nonpartisan center focuses on democracy, especially on voting rights.

Civil Rights Movement: Voting Rights
www.crmvet.org/info/lithome.htm
This website describes what it was like to try to register to vote in different states of the Jim Crow South, with examples of literacy test questions.

FURTHER READING

OurDocuments.gov
ourdocuments.gov
This website features pictures of many original documents that are important to American history, including the history of voting rights, and explains their significance.

The Redistricting Game
www.redistrictinggame.org/index.php
This site is an interactive game where you can redistrict fictional states in different ways.

To Build a Better Ballot
ncase.me/ballot
This website simulates how voting works and how different voting systems work.

INDEX

A

abolitionism, 19, 24, 26
Adams, Abigail, 22–23
African Americans, 5, 8, 11, 16–21, 26, 28, 31–36, 38–40, 48, 52, 54
American Revolution, 8, 10
ancient Greece, 6
Anthony, Susan B., 26–28
Articles of Confederation, 9–10
Asian Americans, 36, 43–45, 54
automatic registration, 56–57

B

black codes, 5, 17
British Bill of Rights, 8
Brown v. Board of Education of Topeka, 35
Burke Act, 43

C

campaign finance, 55
Catt, Carrie Chapman, 28
Chinese Exclusion Act, 43–44
citizenship, 12–13, 17–19, 21, 31, 41–45, 48, 57
Civil Rights Act of 1866, 17–19
civil rights movement, 38–40, 41
Civil War, 5, 14–16, 31, 46

closing polling places, 50, 54
Constitution, US, 8–10, 12, 16, 19, 22, 27, 35–36, 61
constitutional amendments
  Thirteenth, 16–17
  Fourteenth, 19, 26, 31, 33, 41
  Fifteenth, 19–21, 26–27, 31, 41
  Seventeenth, 27
  Nineteenth, 28–31, 41
  Twenty-Third, 45–46
  Twenty-Fourth, 36–38
  Twenty-Sixth, 46–47

D

Dawes Act, 43
Declaration of Sentiments, 24
Douglass, Frederick, 26

E

early voting, 50
Eisenhower, Dwight D., 46
Election Day, 49, 55, 57, 60
elections, early history of, 6–8
electoral vote, 46
exact-match policies, 52–54

F

felons, 4–5, 35–36, 48
For the People Act, 55
fraud, 40, 52, 54, 57

G

gerrymandering, 37, 57–59

78

INDEX

H

homelessness, 5, 52

I

immigrants, 12, 35, 44–45, 55
Indian Citizenship Act, 43
intimidation, 36, 38–39

J

Jim Crow, 5, 33–36, 48, 52
Johnson, Andrew, 16–19
Johnson, Lyndon B., 40

K

Kearney, Belle, 28
Keller, Helen, 28
Kemp, Brian, 52–54
Kennedy, John F., 37
King, Martin Luther, Jr., 40
Ku Klux Klan, 36, 38

L

Latinx Americans, 54
Lewis, John, 40
Lincoln, Abraham, 16–17
literacy tests, 21, 35, 40, 44

M

Madison, James, 10
Magnuson Act, 44–45
mail-in ballots, 59–60
McConnell, Mitch, 55
Meade, Desmond, 5
moral turpitude, 35–36
Motor Voter Act, 48–49

N

National American Woman Suffrage Association (NAWSA), 28
National Voter Registration Act, 48–49
National Woman's Party, 30
Native Americans, 16, 17, 41–43, 52, 60
Naturalization Act of 1790, 13

O

Obama, Barack, 50
online voting, 59

P

Parks, Rosa, 40
Plessy v. Ferguson, 33
poll tax, 35, 36–38, 40, 44
preclearance, 40, 49–50
privacy, 56–57
property ownership, 8, 10–13, 14, 21, 22
protests, 30, 38–40, 46
provisional ballot, 51
purging voter rolls, 35, 50

Q

Quakers, 16, 24

R

ranked-choice voting, 60–61
Reconstruction Act, 17

79

redistricting, 32, 37, 57–59
registration, 4, 5, 35, 38, 40, 48–49, 52–54, 56–57
religion, 10, 12
reservations, 41–43, 60
residency requirements, 40
Roosevelt, Franklin D., 36
Rucho v. Common Cause, 57–58

S

Sayre, Jessie Woodrow Wilson, 30
security, 59
segregation, 5, 33–35
senators, direct election of, 27
Seneca Falls Convention, 24–26
Shelby County v. Holder, 49–50, 54
Sherman, Roger, 9
slavery, 5, 6, 16–19, 31
Stanton, Elizabeth Cady, 24–28
Stevens, Thaddeus, 19
Stone, Lucy, 26–28
Supreme Court, 33–35, 37, 47, 49–50, 52, 54, 57–58

T

tax-paying requirement, 14, 43
temperance movement, 28
territories, 45
three-fifths compromise, 19
Trump, Donald, 50
Truth, Sojourner, 26

V

Vietnam War, 46
voter ID laws, 50, 51–52
voting age, 8, 10, 41, 46–47, 48
voting machines, 59
Voting Rights Act of 1965, 40–41, 47–50

W

Warren, Earl, 35
Washington, DC, 45–46
Wells-Barnett, Ida B., 26
Wilson, Woodrow, 28–30
women, 6, 8, 10–11, 16, 22–30
World War I, 30
World War II, 46